D0612052

Penguin's Big Hill

by Dana Regan

SCHOLASTIC INC.

New York   Toronto   London   Auckland   Sydney
Mexico City   New Delhi   Hong Kong   Buenos Aires

On a cold winter day,
as I sat warm and cozy,
my friends called from outside,
their cheeks bright and rosy.

Get up, you sleepyhead!
Come on, let's go and play!
We're all sliding down
the big, big hill today!

I got out of bed,
and I put on my hat.
I looked out at that hill,
and then I just sat.

That big scary hill
was just way too high.
My friends pulled me up
and said, "Give it a try!"

We marched to the top
in the deep, deep snow.
Then I turned and looked down
at my house far below.

My friends stood still
and so did I.
The big, big hill
was just too high!

Brave Pete went first.
He flew in the air.
He came back down
but we didn't know where.

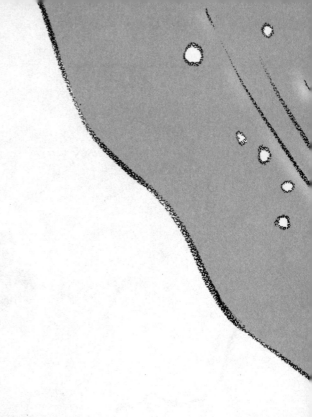

Pat was afraid so
he closed his eyes.
He slid very fast
for someone his size.

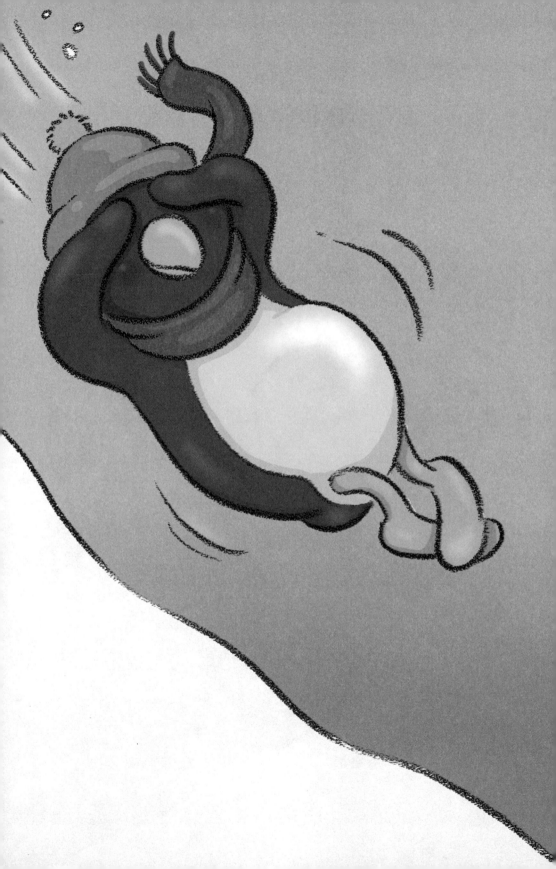

Paula went next,
with a big belly flop.
We all heard her yell,
"How do I stop?"

Penny ran past,
shouting, "Let's go!"
And all we could see
was a big cloud of snow.

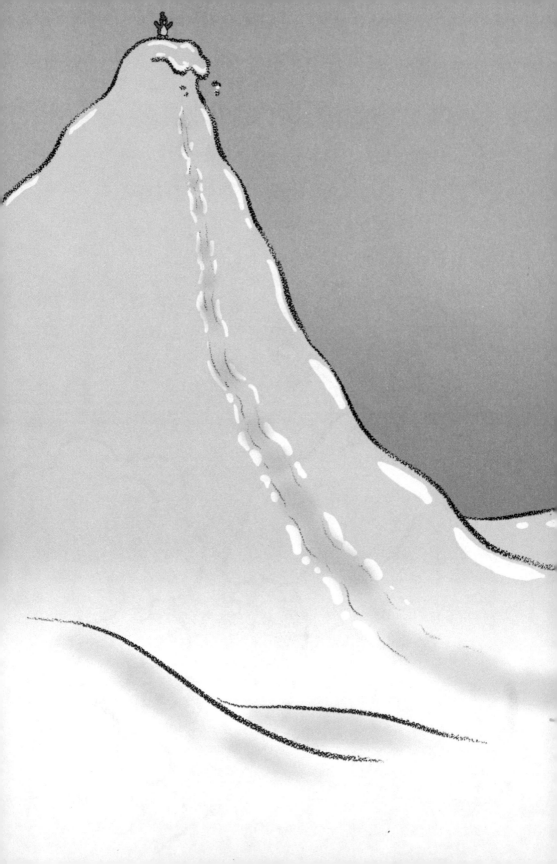

Pammy slid next,
without a sound.
She landed at the bottom
with her up side down.

Now it was my turn.
I blinked and I stared.
My friends didn't know it,
but I was so scared!

I took a deep breath.
I couldn't say no.
I closed my eyes tight,
and I said, "Here I go!"

I slid to the left.
I slid to the right.
I slid past a bear
and hoped he wouldn't bite!

I started rolling over
as I slid down.
I turned into a snowball,
fluffy, white, and round!

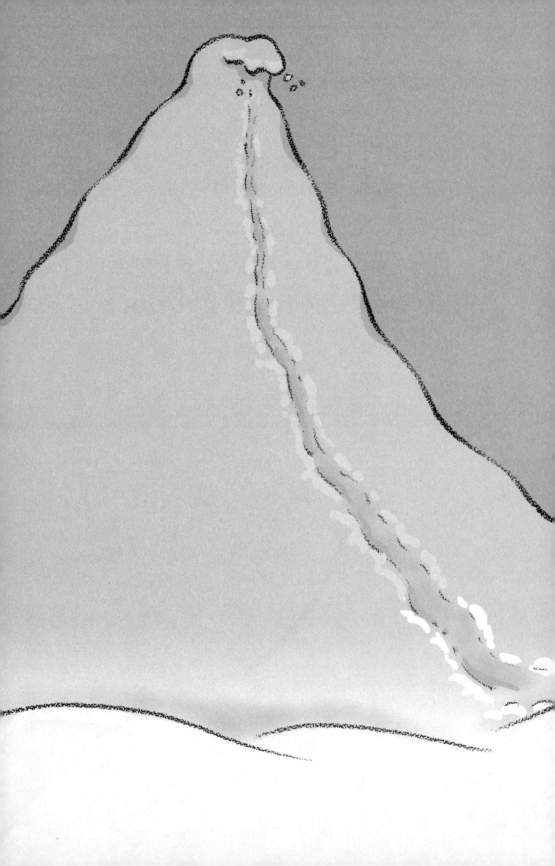

When I got to the bottom,
I rolled to a stop.
I shook off the snow
and looked back at the top.

That big, big hill
wasn't so bad.
I did it by myself
and now I'm glad.

I slid down the
big, big hill today.
Let's all go again!
What do you say?